Mira, Mami I Made The Sun Rise!

A short compilation of poetry written and performed by:

N.P. Harrison

Copyright © 2013 All Rights Reserved
Published by Rumors Have It
New York, NY

ISBN-10: 0615849733
ISBN-13: 978-0-615-84973-7

This collection is dedicated to my twin flame.
The mere knowledge of your existence in the universe
has encouraged my light to shine that much brighter.
Thank you.

Table of Contents:

Step 1 on The Road of Enlightenment:

Step one is always giving of your Self. Until you are ready to do this you cannot possibly call yourself free. The one thing you can absolutely control is already a part of you. There is only one thing truly better than this knowledge. It is in knowing that your Self is free to give to whom/whatever the hell you want. I'm on this planet to spread as much love as I possibly can. It does not mean romantic love. It means love-love. Once again, that 360 degree cypherous cycle, give it-get it-own it-spread it. Today is a good day so enjoy it and be blessed.

"Changes"

I seem to notice that with the changing of time there is a
changing of faces
Left and right I look for the most familiar in dark spaces
Yet, as my eyes begin to focus on the locus of all I want
to see
The reflection in the mirror doesn't even seem to look like
me
I see what I want, and I smell what I fear
But when I open my mouth….what I need, you can't hear
The more you say you've changed is the more you've
stayed the same
It's hard to keep up with these hourly news updates on
my brain
Now tell me once more how much you really really love
me
So that when I turn my back you can forget to add how
your "friends" think your soooo lovely
Those overnight "stays of execution" as a means to
protect,
Well I hope they were worth the reality of neglect
Now maybe I'm crazy, and maybe it's just me
But are the changes in the faces in and out of your door
really so hard to see?
Time is fleeting…..love lasts forever
When I said I didn't trust you….well….Never say Never
I never asked questions, I never told lies
I never pushed you away with tears in your eyes
I never tried to hurt you
I never doubted your intent

I never told you that you were anything less than heaven
sent
See, somebody already broke my heart.....you only had
half a chance
So when you're face changes to your back,
And you think about this last dance
With all the times you've set me up to see if I'd rearrange
Remember, I am the one season that will not change.....

"The Touch"

I missed the chance
Cuz I was too slow
It was a love tap
That was the metaphor for whatever we were
I realized too late
What you brought out for me....
That tingle and tickle of little butterflies
In my tummy came too late!
I didn't realize how your love flowed to me from every
single juice in and on your body
Juices that tasted like honey and smelled like a fine wine
And whose affects numbed my senses nonetheless.
But this time I didn't doze off
And miss my chance like that last time when I was too
slow
Too slow to know just what was there in that touch!
That touch that comes to me and makes me cum
at first mention
But the last time I came too late and missed my chance.
I look at you and I'm lost without my glasses
Cuz I missed my chance when that touch.....
That touch.....
The one I thought was only a second but in looking back I
realize it was much more eternal than that
It blew up and I kept on fallin' like that A.K. kept singing
But I only heard the whispers of the smoke in the air after
that explosive.....
Memory!

The echoes of what I thought was my name was actually
a "Baby, I love you"
And I realized way too late cuz I was deaf from the music
my heart was trying to sing.....
I knew the song but forgot the words and it was too late
when I remembered to sing the words back to you
The words I needed to touch YOUR heart
I knew the song but forgot the words and it was too late
when I remembered to sing the words back to you
The words I needed to touch YOUR soul
I missed the chance
Cuz I was too slow
It was a love tap
That was the metaphor for whatever we were
I realized too late
What you brought out for me....
That tingle and tickle of little butterflies
In my tummy came too late!
I didn't realize how your love flowed to me from every
single juice in and on your body
Juices that tasted like honey and smelled like a fine wine
And whose affects numbed my senses nonetheless
But this time I didn't doze off
And miss my chance like that last time when I was too
slow
Too slow to know just what was there in that touch!
So now I lay here in my bed wide awake after that dose
of heavy
Dreaming.....
Held safe in my mouth I whisper YOUR name.....and
think of you feeling that touch in the dark
In the dark
My touch!

"Untitled #1"

The Dream....
The dream is the essence of the subconscious reality
The dream is the breath that makes me want to do more
than just be
The dream is the beauty whose loves is so true
The dream is me and is of you too
I dream with colors, I dream in smells
I dream in wells of confusion
I dream in my bed, I dream on the train
I dream while sitting at my computer
Your dream is my dream
They are one in the same
And if my dream were your dream
I could give it a new name
Your dream is a smile
Your dream is a kiss
Your dream is a cuddle....one that you will hopefully miss
Your dream is the beginning
My dream is the end
My dream is your completing me
My dream is your complimenting mine
This is the one dream that will last for all time
Sweet dreams...

"Tailor Made"

How do I begin a rhyme
and find a line
to slip and slide
all through your mind
How do I find the words
to lift you up with the birds
and make you feel like the first
only so I could quench my thirst
How do I make love to your soul
Cuz that's my real goal
With you I will grow
It's not spoken but you know
How do I become more than gray matter
What does it take for me to hear your laughter
When I'm around you my heart goes pitter patter
Who can tell me what it is I am after
How do I learn all the things that I yearn
I'm willing to get burned
If my love is not returned
For it's you that makes my head turn
I see stars inside your eyes and oceans in your smile
I could chill on this beach for a long long while

"You Izm"

bless me mother earth for I have sinned
this is my first attempt at a confession
see, when I started, it was innocent enough
I thought my will power was a little bit more tough
With a puff puff here, and a sip sip there,
And golden angels whispering in my left ear
Telling me secrets of a past best left unremembered
I never thought of ties needing ever to be severed
My dealer was divine,
Teaching me lessons on how to stop time
My dealer was in disguise,
Only masked by my blood shot eyes
She handed me that unsterile sword
And taught me how to put on my armor, a cord
a heavy sleep that only comes after a night of intense
mind/soul
fuckin'
with my shield of dreams
and my wax made wings
I flew as high as that bird in the sky
Waking up in a cold sweat
I remembered my dealer and that infamous bet
Will you be mine? She said to me
Spoken through words only a true hustler could see
And that powerful drug laced with love and pains
Made its way through just about all of my veins
I could feel my life slippin' away
Withdrawing and weak, but unafraid of the day
She held me close and said I'd be fine
All of our bodies die, it just takes time

So now that I'm here and ready to come correct
I know that this penance won't gain me respect
The mind was willing but the body was unable
The bitch kicked my ass without once leaving the table
And I'm speaking to you behind soulless eyes
Warning you....about the danger of lies

"Untitled #2"

This is the hour of my discontent
With romantic letters of disrespect
One love lost in order to save another
One love lost to spare a mother
Children not yet birthed or conceived
With actions of love, it is still not believed
I tried to tell you over and over
But you insisted on letting, all of my words hover
I love you, I love you not, all twisted in a sick game
Although it was simple, you couldn't pronounce my name
Lost in a storm of repression and depression
I have to let go of this silly obsession
I'm not sure what to do
Whether to let go or continue
It doesn't really matter, cuz you're doing you
At once I felt freed
From crap and misdeeds
But you've seemed to recapture
The exquisite pain of enrapture
Maybe it's worth it, but then again no
Maybe it's fate, and our stars are telling us so
I wish I could hold on to all the things that remind me of
you
But what is there left: pictures? A brush? Maybe even a
shoe?
I'm telling you this just to let you know
My love was never a game, or some stupid puppet show

The choices we make, they reflect who we are
If you're choice is to be a bird, you shouldn't fly so very
far
Long distant relationships have nothing to do with this
It's the problems that ensue, they are so easy to miss

Step 2 on The Road of Enlightenment:

This step is very important. It is the ability and power to accept love from someone else. That is genuine, because you are a child of God and you deserve to be loved purely. So many times we get caught up in relationships that appear to be loving and they are truly not. We sometimes think, "Well.....I guess it's love". I mean what!?! LOVE IS LOVE IS LOVE IS....it exists whether you want it to or not and she always needs a heart in which to live.....Trust me as I say this: when someone loves you, you will know it and you'd never ever have to doubt it. Having the trust to do that can be the biggest challenge but if you go back and review step 1, you'll be fine. Most importantly, don't forget to love yourself first. If you don't love you, who do you think should?

"Niccas 4 Lyfe"

I lost my Nicca 4 Lyfe last night
My Nicca committed soulful suicide
My Nicca gave up all the Nicca ways and got bitched by
a dog
Yeah, try and tell me you don't know the song
Love and satisfaction could not keep my Nicca
And cuz my Nicca got bored the gap grew bigger
Sold me out like the weakest slave on the plantation
Cuz the only thing Nicca couldn't resist went by the name
of Temptation
Temptation had a power that even Jesus couldn't save
And even I couldn't hear the echoes from that walking
grave
Temptation taught classes at the school of hard knocks
And my Nicca was teacher's pet
The lesson plan for day one was already set
See cuz "every little thing that we do
Should be between me and you
And if your Nicca only knew
She'd lose all her trust in you"
My Nicca studied real hard and got high grades
Temptation got to lay in the bed my Nicca made
Now the lesson I've learned from the whole situation
Is a hoe's a hoe and that includes temptation
My "Nicca 4 Lyfe" I will remember forever
But to love another Nicca, I'd have to say "never"
Fuck getting' played it's not what I'm about
My Nicca knew I wasn't a game, but was the last to find
out
So the moral of my story about Niccas 4 Lyfe
It's when you're huggin' Judas and Brutus, keep your eye
out for the knife!

"A Love Letter"

Dear Cupid,

I'm writing to let you know that I received your arrow today. I just wanted to say thank you very much but you've got the wrong person! I appreciate all your efforts in bringing me love but there are just some things you wouldn't understand. See, I've been down this road too many times to let myself get caught up in some mess. I get tired of hearing all the excuses cuz I've heard them all before. Me and my heart have been to hell and back with all to show for it, a lousy T-shirt. With all the baby's mama drama, damn I love you so much it hurts, and I wish you were you-know-whos piling up outside my door, the last thing I need is your long assed narrow arrow trying to pierce me through my soul. So, save the drama for YOUR mama and kindly take back this crap that's making me bleed all over my carpet. The shipping and handling is free of charge, there are no COD's, layaway plans, or credit checks necessary. Have a beautiful day!

Sincerely,

Me

"The Journey of a Poem"

The poem can last forever, or for just a moment
The poem is as simple as a breath
Or as complex as the person it stems from
I am the person
I am the breath
I am the moment
But must important
I am forever

"Untitled #3"

I'm dreaming dreams of raisins in the sun
While watching children of a lesser god making angels in
the snow
With wings spread out as far as that bird in the sky
Cuz Nina's Blues don't move me anymore
See I know what happens with dreams deferred
I've taken mental pictures of eternity
That seems to last the life span of a butterfly
But one monkey don't stop no show
And that house on Mango Street will be there forever
That sacred place in that sacred space holds more
breath than I have in my chest
But never fear, cuz when there's no room in hell, the
dead will walk the earth
To teach us the truths are eyes have been too blind to
see

"Taste the Rainbow"

Have you ever met a girl who wanted to come into your world
And taste the rainbow?
She wanted to be down and have fam in every town
And taste the rainbow?
She wanted to leave the boys behind, and have the hardest stud she could find
And taste the rainbow?
Eh, did she want to sport the flag…but u betta had never call her fag
And taste the rainbow?
Could she only comes out at night and have your happy ass meet her down the block
Or when ya'll got to the club, you lost her until about 3 o'clock
And taste the rainbow?
See now bi girls are funny, but straight girls are more fun
Cuz honestly, and this is real, they like anything that makes them cum
And taste the rainbow?
Now the stubborn ones will always try and go back
But not until after this rainbow has tasted her back

"Untitled #4"

Here I am chillin' just writin' a few silly rhymes
And swimming in my thoughts of you trying not to capsize
See, I'm floatin' in tainted waters of the words you so
easily spoke
Tell me playa, has my mind turned into a game or did my
heart just get broke
I don't know which way is up and my down is just a
mystery
And the last time I had a good fuck?
Yo, that shit seems like ancient history
Damn it's been awhile since I've played that crazy love
game
But with all these gorgeous females out here, yo my
name? I'm about to change....
Hold up playa, don't get your shit twisted
You had a good chance but you fucked up and missed it
I still remember the little things you used to do that were
cute
But take a number shorty, cuz my heart just gave you the
boot
Since me your selection has not been very tight
They would never be able to do what I would do AND do
it all night
But eh, I'm not hating
I can see your trying your luck at dating
The easy part is loving, the hardest part is living

Step 3 on The Road of Enlightenment:

This step is important because it involves action. We find ourselves here all the time. We know there are things we want to do in life and things we wish we could do that just do not seem feasible. This step involves GETTING OFF YOUR ASS. I know, it's tough. Right now this economy is really really bad. However, if you're used to strugglin' and hustlin', you're already ahead of the game. Sit down and write down where you want to be in life, feasible or not, in 10 years. Then make your brainstorm visible with paper and pen and what it is you would need to get you there. After all of that, get rid of the nonsense filling up your pages and see what's left. Absolutely everything is doable. But are you willing to put in work? Go back to school, run a business, compete in the Olympics. F&*k it, like NIKE says, "just do it". Only you can hold yourself back from anything. If you're blaming others then you will continue to be a prisoner. Prisoners don't roam free but they do work for free. I'll borrow a line from Mos Def as a solid mantra, "I'm a workin' person, I put in work, I work with purpose"....

"Untitled #5"

Today it's "eye for an eye"
Tomorrow it's "turn the other cheek"
I need to get my shit together cuz the truth could change
by the middle of next week
I wanna put down my weapons and give up the fight
I wanna put down my weapons and return to life
They say I'm an American, can someone tell me what
that means?
Cuz I remember them sayin' all I eat are watermelons
and collard greens
I'm not good enough to take your daughter out, and show
her some good times
But I'm the first one you ask to get behind enemy lines

"The Secrets We Keep"

The secrets we keep
They run kind of deep
Deep down in the subconscious, they find a way to linger
You can point your finger at me, and I could just give you
the finger
Your secret's 10 years old, while mine is 23
Were you even gonna tell me that your secret is a he?
You have another baby's mother, and a woman is my
lover
The secrets we keep
Yo, they run kind of deep
So let me get this right, and make sure it's all straight
Now I have a new little brother, and he's even my
namesake?
Mom took my secret a lot better than she took yours
When bad things happen, yo I swear I think they happen
in fours
I broke up with wifey, my best friend lied
I had to quit my job, and in my head my own father died
I never use the word hate, and for 17 years it fit you to a
tee
We lived in the same house all of my life, and you still
don't even know me
The secrets we keep
See, they run kind of deep
You don't know the name of the university I go to
And I still have no clue what it is at your job that you do
I'm feelin' this piece, I'm feelin' it real tight
Did you know that I perform, or that I even had a mind to
write?
The secrets that we keep
Yeah, they run kind of deep!

"The Night I Knocked on Heaven's Door"

The night I knocked on heaven's door I didn't know just
what to expect
I could never fathom the beauty of the angel that came
out to inspect
She weighed me, measured me, and tried to find me
wanting…
But as hard as it was for her to realize, to find my equal
would leave her haunting
She smiled and was polite as she could fake
She kept trying to test to see if she'd made another
mistake
I'd traveled all this way and thought I found my New
Edition "Candy Girl"
And ended up finding my New Kid on the Block
"Popsicle"
Sweet, juicy, wet …but ice cooooold…and gave me brain
freeze
My nose had a little tickle and I started to sneeze
So instead of standing in line to be the next bungee
jumping fool
I turned around and hopped on the green line making my
way back to school
That night I knocked on heaven's door was much longer
than it should have been
And on my way back home I tried to recollect just how
many commandments I'd broken
This angel was too perfect…complete in too many ways
I knew with her conviction, her time in heaven wouldn't
last but a few days
She wanted to know everything about life

She was smart and she was true
And as sharp as a knife
She didn't know how powerful she honest and truly could
be
My sweet angel didn't have wings cuz she gave hers to
those who couldn't see
She could fly and touch the stars in the sky
But she chose to stay and be made lesser by one
confused guy
He told her that he loved her but that she'd never
compare
And the words that he spoke were written in her stare
This one small angel was truly a queen
But by her unruly prince, her crown could not be seen
And that night I knocked on heaven's door
I could not imagine the royalty in store
Impressed by even a glimpse of this empress
I walk the long road home far away from heaven's door

"Why Do You Want to See Me Cry?"

A Convo with TaZ (this is a work in progress....just like us!)
Cuz I want to be the one who makes it better, wipes your tears
Do u realize that there is no music in the room when you're not around?
Do u know that it always rains when I can`t see your face?
Do u know that if I could reach up into the sky I`d pick a star and give it to you
while asking u to be my forever valentine?
Do u know that when I feel your heart beat I can hear the laughter of our kids
bump bump
bump bump
bump bump bump
So at the end of the road right....
And u look back with fond remembrance
Where will I be?
Next to you?
Or down the history line?
"It all depends on what roads we`re both at in life and how much you want or want not to be on that history line."
I want to be on the line that has u on it!
Not behind nor in front
Right next to you!
I want to grow with u and even though I`m mad old, there`s still growing that needs to be done!
U willin` to grow with me?
U willin` to take that plunge?

U willin` to let go?
U willin` to learn to fly?
U willin` to test your speed?
U willin` to find your limits and exceed?
U willin` to be the ultimate poem?
U willin` to be the inspired art?
Cuz there are few words to describe what I`m feelin`
Few words that could ever amount to what I SHOULD
say
No metaphor could truly break it down for you...

"A New Peace"

Would you mind if I spent a little time with this here rhyme
And ravaged your mind as I flow to the next line?
This sexual intoxication is just a manifestation of my
obligation to loving you right.... riiiiiight...
I watch you slowly moving across the room and my eyes
zoom just hoping you`ll get here soon cuz...slow motion
is cool but no friend of mine....
Would you mind if I enticed your body lines and glow by
the light of your eyes?
I know you`re speaking but in my mind I`m thinking how
you`d taste
So let`s make haste
This time I won`t waste
In taking you to my place and playing R & B Jams while
you`re singing operatic melodies
You said you were my Goddess when I called you my
Queen,
And cuz you ruled the universe, you didn`t have time for
an earthly thing
You can c umm hot or you can c umm sweet, just as long
as you c umm.
Cuz even though it`s almost over, I`ve only just begun.....

"Crossroads"

I'm at the pivot point
The centrifugal force has played her tricks
Now I'm in the zone of motionlessness
The feeling of numb has subsided
Maybe the eternal freeze is over
Maybe the sun has freed her victimized daughter
Maybe this moon child has finally found the power to
move the tides
Here at the center there are many different directions
No longer do I have to find my map
The directions are wrong
I know this path by heart
I've been here before
She knows where she's going
I am her and she is me
We've been on this journey together
My pen is free my mind is on cruise
I'm writing….look I'm writing
I'm spittin', the fire is back
The flame is lit
My mission is sure…

Step 4 on The Road of Enlightenment:

I've always had difficulties with the concept of forgiveness. I honestly believe that I've never forgiven anyone for anything. For me, to forgive someone is to absolve them from all accountability of their actions. In doing so it negates the factual nature of their actions and the results of those actions. To forgive someone means that you are saying what they have done is ok and is acceptable if they ask politely and sincerely for it, should be given. As a Catholic I was taught that this is what God wants us to do. Confess your sins, ask sincerely for forgiveness and so shall it be forevermore. If you give give give you get get get. Unfortunately there is no forgetting when it comes to forgiving. We will always be fearful that whatever happened that hurt us in the first place would possibly happen again. It's human nature. We become stagnant because we are deeply concerned about what the future has in store for us and don't quite clearly press forward. Our steps are somewhat hindered even if it's by the slightest degree. I believe in letting go. In this way I acknowledge I've been wronged. I accept that the other person is truly sorry if in fact they are and I move forward. By letting go the actions no longer harm me or my feelings and allow me the freedom of flight without fear. Forgiveness is inherently an instant process. Someone says "I'm sorry". Someone says "I forgive you" and then all is supposed to be well from that moment. Letting go could take a lifetime. It is a skill that needs nurturing and is a necessity in building relationships.
Forgiveness is an ideal that if the same action of wrongdoing were repeated may not be given a 2nd time. It's fleeting. Letting go instantly makes the same repeated action someone else's problem.

"Soul Mate"

I was running faster and faster trying to grab ahold of the
corner at the edge of the earth
But I got lost
And in the distance I heard the sweet sound of your
name being whispered
My heart stopped before my feet did and as I followed the
song with my ear
I started to cry
See cuz my soul remembered more than I
And once again I could not resist your temptation
But wait, no hesitation
Your sweet temple, your sacred kingdom is calling out to
me
"I AM THE ONE WHO WILL SAVE!"
And as I stand here being enticed by your….one part
harmony
I'm reminded of a story once told to me about life
He said that I was only a shadow and that I was just a
poor player
Strutting and fretting my hour upon this stage
And I said,
"YOU LIE!
I WILL NOT GO GENTLE!
I WILL RAGE!
I WILL RAGE!
I WILL RAGE!"
And even now as your melody
Enraptures me
I find myself floating away to a place where the sea
meets the sky

To a place where the trees are babies reaching up to a
suckling mother
To a place where that first come hither look in the garden
Was actually a deafening cry to share one
Glorious
Intense
Warm
Wet
Juicy
Moment of satisfaction
So, slowly very slowly I open my eyes to see this cotton
candy dream my heart and mind have created for me
And this smile on my face is not a blush from a first
encounter with a crush
This smile on my face is from a little taste of the sugar
you put in my bowl
What's the matter mama, come on
Save my soul
I want some sugar in my bowl!

"Untitled #6"

Your love should be named eternal for it carries me high
into oblivion
So high that the darkness pervades my mind and my soul
is left silently screaming
There is no one around me but you slapping me into
consciousness of self
Your love has awakened in me a whirlwind of passion
Flowing and blowing I'm grappling onto the billion ton
walls of my mind
Fingers bleeding, tears dropping, limbs getting tired of
holding on for dear life
I'm tryin', I'm tryin' but my security blankets tryin' harder
sayin'
"Nik, it won't hurt! Let go! Let go!"
and the only response I can muster up is,
"But….But….
I CAN'T EVEN THINK STRAIGHT!!!!
NO….Oh my God, I'm fallin'!
I'm fallin'!
HELLLLLLLLLLLLLLLLLP!!!!!!
And as tweety gets down to the widdow piddy that cried
all the way home
I'm gone
No longer myself but that of another
Once used and abused, now new and improved
The conflicted part, being played by this heart, is singing
sweet melodies
That Nina could only sing about in her dreams
And your love….
Like the song "Remains the Same"

This pleasurable torture of mind versus heart,
Makes me anticipate our erotic start
My cancer, your aquarius...of the same ocean...
Where the depths know no bounds
Where the greens and blues combine to form smiles that
stretch from the
Sahara Desert to the lost city of Atlantis
Can I get lost in your smile?
Can I quench my thirst as I gently place my lips on your
Tigris and Euphrates Rivers?
I'll ask you once again but the question's never ending....
Can I keep you?

"Peaches and Cream"

Juices oozing
Seducing
Confusing
Inducing woozing
"Gimmie some head!"
Spread across the bed
Lemme see some red
And the ink to your lead
Lead to my ink
Sprawled across the sink
Too hot to think
But your close to the brink
So we'll go with the flow
Cuz I suck but don't blow
Act like you know
Tu papi chulo fa sho
Hands tied behind your back
Give that ass a little smack
One leg on my lap
The other hangin' from a rack
Clit to lips,
Lips to clit
Lovin' your coatin' of cherry flavored chapstick

"I'm Taking My Black Back"

Ain't no sunshine when she's gone
There's just grey clouds everyday
Ain't no sunshine when she's gone
And she's always gone too long
Anytime she goes away
I'm taking my black back
Do you think you can handle that?
You sent her away when you came into the picture
You said I couldn't have her as long as I was with you
I'm missin' her taste
I'm missin' her smell
I'm missin' all that she meant to me
She's a lot more faithful than you turned out to be
She was my friend
She was my lover
She stayed around longer than any other
She was my dawg in times of doubt
She was the one who tried to console me when I wanted
to kick you out
Remember that day you got on your knees and cried?
Well she already told me you had something to hide
She'd let off her steam to me
Well it smelled more like smoke
She reminded me of our past love
And said that this one was a joke
I want my black back
Do you think you can handle that?
Don't tell me you're jealous
Of what we used to have?

We'd make love outside
Sometimes even in the bath
I used to put my tongue on her tip
And my lips on her....
Well, that was a long time ago
But if we had taped it
It would have been some show
The way we went at it was like an Olympic sport
It was a hell of a lot better than you and your Newport
I'm taking my black back
Do you think you can handle that?
There ain't no sunshine when she's gone
There's just grey clouds everyday
Ain't no sunshine when she's gone
And she's always gone too long
Anytime she goes away...

"U"

As the sun sets
I'm thinkin'of you
And drinkin' of you
While reeking of you
Numerous nights seducing you
In hopes of consuming you
And no thoughts of losing you
I find myself missing you
Lost deep in thoughts of kissing you
My days spent swimming in you.

"LALALALALA"

I wanna do dirty dirty dirty things to you
I mean not just dirty.
Absolutely raunchy.
I wanna stroke you in places you've never been looked at
I wanna kiss you in places you can't even reach
You feel me?
Yeah you do....
Tell me how good it feels when my eyes wander
anywhere they wanna go
All over your booooody
You wanna what?
My tongue huh?
Baby you not even ready yet
My eyes ain't got nothing' on my tongue.....
See?
You didn't even realize how many times and how deep I
wrote my name through you
Baby why you stutterin'?
It's like that?
You feel me...
Don't you?
Dirty dirty dirty and very very messy things
It's all good ma
I'm prepped for clean up
Not one drop spent and wasted
From my lips to the gates of heaven
Love like this burns like ice
Melting between your legs and forming something new
Of course I'm your Sugar Bear
And you're my Gumdrop

Just drippity drippin' the moment I snap my fingers
Ms. Phee whisperin' your secrets when you're not paying
attention
Don't worry baby, I got this
Letting go isn't an option
So you better hold on tight
And just remember this all started with me
Getting real close to you
And gently putting my lips
Near to your ear
Quietly whispering
"lalalalala"

www.ingramcontent.com/pod-product-compliance
Lightning Source LLC
Chambersburg PA
CBHW071224130626
46555CB00004B/1840